biy

For Maisie -
C.C.

British Library Cataloguing Publication Data
A catalogue record of this book is available from the British Library

HB ISBN 0 340 743859
PB ISBN 0 340 743867

First hb edition published 1999
First pb edition published 1999

1 3 5 7 9 10 8 6 4 2

Published by Hodder Children's Books,
a division of Hodder Headline plc,
338 Euston Road, London NW1 3BH

Designed by Dawn Apperley

Printed in Hong Kong

Don't do that, Kitty Kilroy!

Cressida Cowell

h
Hodder
Children's
Books

A division of Hodder Headline plc

All day long Kitty's mum says:

Don't do that, Kitty Kilroy!

When Kitty puts her feet up on the sofa:

Don't do that, Kitty Kilroy!

When Kitty eats food that is bad for her teeth:

Don't do that, Kitty Kilroy!

When Kitty makes a big mess of the sitting room:

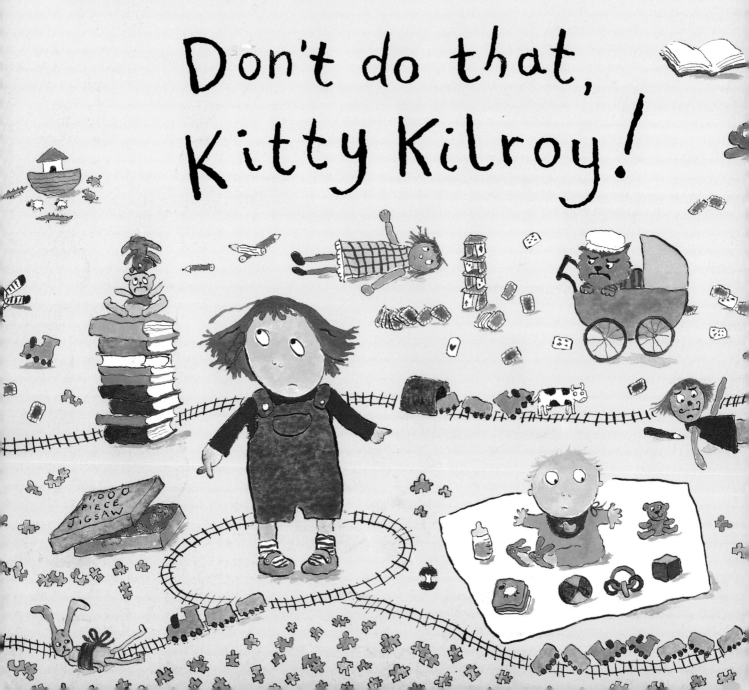

Don't do that, Kitty Kilroy!

One day Kitty had had enough:

Why don't you go away and let me do what I want?

So Kitty's mother DID go away …

. . . and Kitty got to do what she wanted.

She wore pyjamas all day long.

She ate nothing but cold cereal and ice-cream . . .

. . . which gave her lots of energy.

She watched television for hours and hours.

She rang up all her friends . . .

. . . and invited them round to help her mess up the sitting room . . .

. . . and stay up way past their bedtimes.

After a while it was no fun anymore.

Suddenly there was a sound at the door and . . .

... it was Kitty's mother.

What do you want to do now, Kitty Kilroy?

Kitty's mother sent Kitty's friends
home to their mothers.

Kitty's mum washed Kitty's face.
And she gave Kitty some medicine
to make her feel better.

Sleep tight, Kitty Kilroy

She put Kitty to bed, which was just what Kitty wanted.

Until tomorrow of course ...